DATE DUE		

For

Diana Mann, because.

Iona Opie

For

Amelia and Amy.

Rosemary Wells

BANBURY CROSS
9

HERE COMES MOTHER GOOSE

edited by

IONA OPIE

illustrated by

ROSEMARY WELLS

CANDLEWICK PRESS
CAMBRIDGE, MASSACHUSETTS

Here comes Mother Goose

Long ago, when the troubadours still roamed the lanes of Europe, a wise old bird called Mother Goose began to save small fragments of the songs that people most enjoyed. (She was called Frau Gosen in those days.)

As she wandered, she overheard men singing as they worked in the fields, and women singing as they rocked their babies to sleep, and she kept the songs warm under her wings. She listened to children at their play, and to grandads in chimney corners, reciting the sagacious distichs they had learned from *their* grandfathers. She invented rhymes to help babies find out where their eyes and noses are, and rhymes to help older children learn their numbers and the alphabet.

Nonsense verses she liked, and clever riddles. And more than all the others she liked the songs that run in people's heads and make them skip instead of walk, or dance around a room all on their own. This immortal lady has never stopped collecting; from every century she has stashed away the best.

When Mother Goose discovered how much *nicer* children are when fed on nursery rhymes, she published the rhymes in little books and added illustrations. The first, *Tommy Thumb's Pretty Song Book,* 1744, measured but 3 x 1¾ inches, and was adorned with thirty-six miniature engravings. Now, 250 years or so later, we have a book big enough to hide behind in a railway carriage, and as full of color and revelry as anyone could long for on a gray winter's day. Rosemary Wells has created a host of memorable characters: cozy mother rabbits, cheeky ducklings, resolute and responsible dogs, adventurous cats. A family of guinea pigs act as clowns. They turn cartwheels and stand on their heads (an upside-down guinea pig is called a "pinny gig"). Ten of them, below, persuade us that topsy-turvy and frack-to-bont is the most delightful way to live: their names are

Impty, Dimpty, Tipsy-tee,
Oka-poka, Dominee;
Hocus-pocus, Dominocus,
Om, Pom, and Tosh.

Iona Opie

Mabel, Mabel,
strong and able,
Take your elbows
off the table.

Contents

One-ery, two-ery, tickery, ten,
Bobs of vinegar, gentlemen.
A bird in the air,
a fish in the sea,
A bonny wee lassie
came singing to me.

Chapter One
1, 2, Buckle My Shoe

Buckle my shoe;

Knock at the door;

Pick up sticks;

Lay them straight;

A big fat hen.

Mary, Mary, quite contrary,
How does your garden grow?
With silver bells and cockleshells,
And pretty maids all in a row.

Hot cross buns, hot cross buns;
One a penny poker,
Two a penny tongs,
Three a penny fire shovel,
Hot cross buns.

I had a sausage,

a bonny

bonny sausage,

I put it

in the oven

for my tea.

I went down
the cellar,
to get the
salt and pepper,
And the sausage
ran after me.

Bobby Shaftoe's gone to sea,
Silver buckles at his knee;
He'll come back and marry me,
Bonny Bobby Shaftoe.

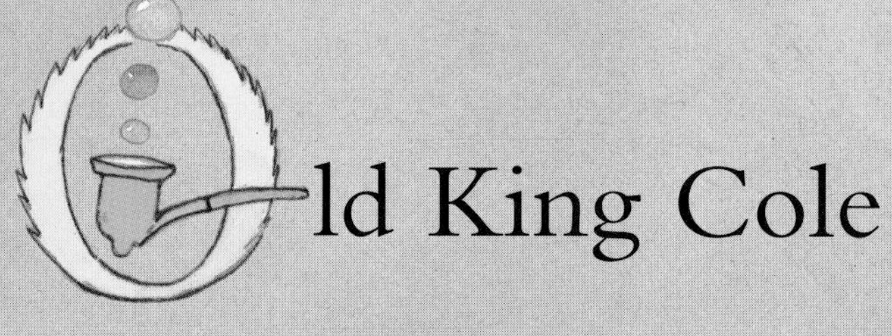

Old King Cole
Was a merry old soul
And a merry old soul was he;

He called for his pipe
And he called for his bowl
And he called for his fiddlers three.

Cross-patch, draw the latch,
Sit by the fire and spin;
Take a cup, and drink it up,
Then call your neighbors in.

I had a little hen
The prettiest ever seen;
She washed up the dishes,
And kept the house clean.

She went to the mill
To fetch me some flour,
And always got home
In less than an hour.

Brush hair,
brush,

The men are gone

to plow,

If you want to brush

your hair,

Brush your

hair now.

Jelly on a plate,
Jelly on a plate,
Wibble, wobble, wibble, wobble,
Jelly on a plate.

Sausage in a pan,
Sausage in a pan,
Frizzle, frazzle, frizzle, frazzle,
Sausage in a pan.

Baby on the floor,
Baby on the floor,
Pick him up, pick him up,
Baby on the floor.

What are little girls made of, made of?
What are little girls made of?

Frogs and snails and puppy-dogs' tails,
That's what little girls are made of.

What are little boys made of, made of?

What are little boys made of?

Sugar and spice and all things nice,

That’s what little boys are made of.

Simple Simon met a pieman,
Going to the fair;
Says Simple Simon to the pieman,
Let me taste your ware.

Says the pieman to Simple Simon,
Show me first your penny;
Says Simple Simon to the pieman,
Indeed, I have not any.

Will you come to my party,
will you come?
Bring your own bread and butter
and a bun;
Mrs. Murphy will be there,
Tossing peanuts in the air,
Will you come to my party,
will you come?

R.S.V.P.

I asked my mother for fifty cents,

To see the elephant jump the fence,

He jumped so high,

He reached the sky,

And didn't come back till the Fourth of July.

Red sky at night,
Shepherd's delight;

Red sky in the morning,
Shepherd's warning.

Chapter Two

Old Mother Hubbard

Old Mother Hubbard
Went to the cupboard,
To fetch her poor dog a bone;
But when she got there
The cupboard was bare
And so the poor dog had none.

She went to the fishmonger's
To buy him some fish;
But when she came back
He was licking the dish.

She went to the fruiterer's

To buy him some fruit;

But when she came back

He was playing the flute.

I'm Dusty Bill
From Vinegar Hill,
Never had a bath
And I never will.

Early in the morning at eight o'clock
You can hear the postman's knock;
Up jumps Ella to answer the door,
One letter, two letters, three letters, four!

FOOF
FOOF
YANGA
POSTED
YANGA
FOOF
FOOF
FOOF
AMBIDEXTROS
YANGA

LAND OF THE MID-DAY MOON
POST CARD
SALTINA
SALTINA
6
8
POSTED
Hello!
Having a wonderful
time. Wish you were here!
Love,
S. Claus
CANCELLED
AIR MAIL
Ella Bunny
1 Whitehall Avenue
Deal 7053

REPUBLICA FOOF
1P
FOOF
FOOF
AIR
Miss Ella Bunny
1 Whitehall Ave
Deal 7053
SPIRITUS DENTUS

Easter Bunny. Room 41
HOTEL
SOCRATES
1ST CLASS
AMBIDEXTROS
AIR MAIL
AIR MAIL
Ms. Ella Bunny
1 Whitehall Ave.
Deal, 7053
KOPI

Ma Goose
Hotel des Palmes
Yanga
YANGA
YANGA
Miss Ella Bunny
1 Whitehall Ave.
Deal 7053
URGENT
AIRMAIL
PAR AVION

My Aunt Jane,

She came from France,

To teach to me the polka dance;

First the heel,

And then the toe,

That's the way

The dance should go.

POLKA
L R
BOY
L R
GIRL

CAFÉ des POIS
F
C

Christopher Columbus
was a very great man,
He sailed to America
in an old tin can.
The can was greasy,
And it wasn't very easy,
And the waves grew higher,
and higher,
and higher.

Santa Maria
BAKED BEANS
PINTA
VITAMIN
CUSTARD

Wake up, baby, day's a-breaking,

Peas in the pot and a hoe-cake baking.

Diddle, diddle, dumpling,
my son John,
Went to bed with his trousers on;

One shoe off,
and one shoe on,

Diddle, diddle, dumpling,
my son John.

Twinkle, twinkle,

little star,

How I wonder what you are!

Up above the world so high,

Like a diamond in the sky.

Chapter Four
I Danced with the Girl

I danced with the girl
With a hole in her stocking,
And her heel kept a-rocking,
And her heel kept a-rocking;
I danced with the girl
With a hole in her stocking,
We danced by the light of the moon.

TANGO
START
START
BOY
L
R
GIRL
L
R

Bluebells, cockleshells,

Evie, ivie, over,

Mother's in the kitchen

Doing a bit of stitching,

Baby's in the cradle

Playing with a rattle,

A rickety stick, a walking stick,

One, two, three.

Mademoiselle
she went to the well,
She didn't forget her
soap and towel;
She washed her hands,
she wiped them dry,
She said her prayers,
and jumped up high.

Tinker, tailor,

Soldier, sailor,

Rich man, poor man,

Plowboy,

Thief.

Peter, Peter, pumpkin eater,

Had a wife and couldn't keep her;

He put her in a pumpkin shell

And there he kept her very well.

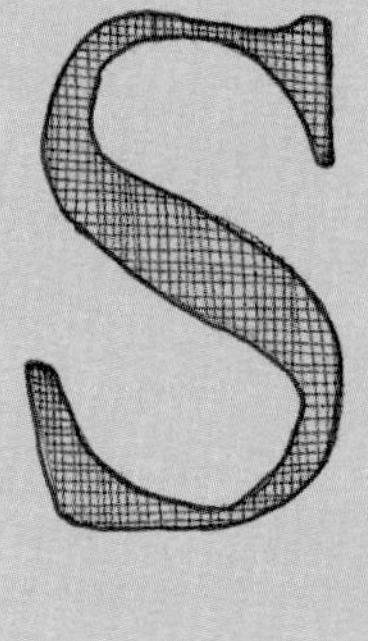

ieve my lady's oatmeal, grind my lady's flour,

Put it in a chestnut, let it stand an hour.

My father's a king and my mother's a queen,

My two little sisters are dressed all in green.

Sukey, you shall
be my wife
And I will tell you why:
I have got a little pig,
And you have got a sty;

I have got a
dun cow,
And you can make good cheese;
Sukey, will you marry me?
Say Yes, if you please.

The Queen of Hearts
She made some tarts,
All on a summer's day;

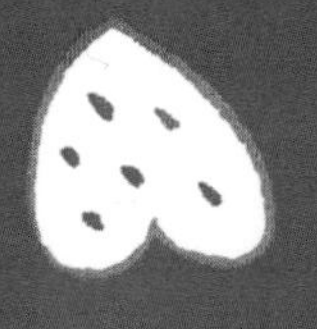

The Knave of Hearts
He stole the tarts,
And took them clean away.

Down in the valley where the green grass grows,

There's a pretty maiden she grows like a rose;

She grows, she grows, she grows so sweet,

She sings for her true love across the street.

Tommy, Tommy, will you marry me?

Yes, love, yes, love, at half past three.

Ice cakes, spice cakes, all for tea,

We'll have our wedding at half past three.

Ride a cock horse
To Banbury Cross,
To see what Tommy can buy;
A penny white loaf,
A penny white cake,
And a two-penny apple pie.

PIE!
2p
CAKE
1p
BREAD
1p

s I was walking through the City,

Half past eight o'clock at night,

There I met a Spanish lady,

Washing out her clothes at night.

First she rubbed them, then she scrubbed them,

Then she hung them out to dry,

Then she laid her hands upon them

Said: I wish my clothes were dry.

 El Jabón  La Luna  La Camisa

Away down east,

away down west,

Away down Alabama,

The only girl that I love best

Her name is Susianna.

Come, crow! Go, crow!

Baby's sleeping sound,

And the wild plums grow in the jungle,

Only a penny a pound.

Only a penny a pound, Baba,

Only a penny a pound.

There was a man of double deed
Sowed his garden full of seed.
When the seed began to grow,
'Twas like a garden full of snow.

Index of First Lines

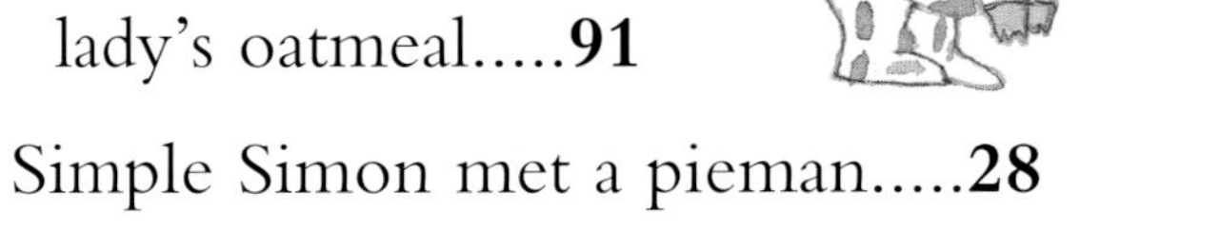

First U.S. edition 1999

Library of Congress Cataloging-in-Publication Data

Here comes Mother Goose / edited by Iona Opie ; illustrated by
Rosemary Wells. — 1st U.S. ed.
p. cm.
Summary: Presents more than sixty traditional nursery rhymes,
including "Old Mother Hubbard," "I'm a Little Teapot," and "One,
Two, Buckle My Shoe," accompanied by illustrations of various animals.
ISBN 0-7636-0683-9
1. Nursery rhymes. 2. Children's poetry. [1. Nursery rhymes.]
I. Opie, Iona Archibald. II. Wells, Rosemary, ill. III. Mother Goose.
PZ8.3.H4201 1999
398.8 — dc21 99-14256

4 6 8 10 9 7 5

Printed in Hong Kong

This book was typeset in M Bembo.
The illustrations were done in watercolor, ink, and other media.

Candlewick Press
2067 Massachusetts Avenue
Cambridge, Massachusetts 02140